CAESAR, WHO'S HE?

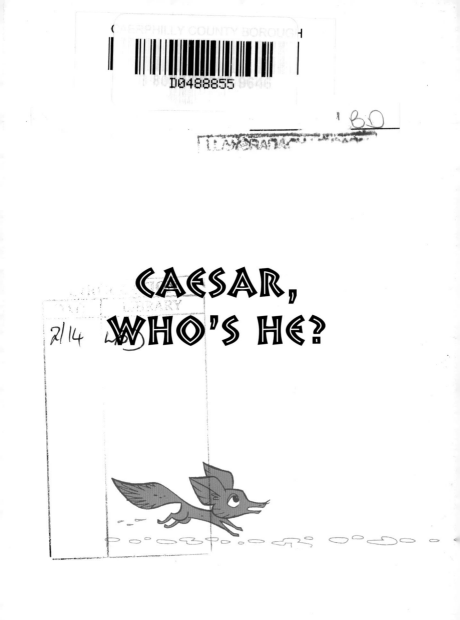

First published in France by Éditions Flammarion MMIV

This edition published by Scribo MMXI,
Scribo, a division of Book House, an imprint of
The Salariya Book Company
25 Marlborough Place, Brighton, BN1 1UB

www.book-house.co.uk
www.salariya.com
www.scribobooks.com

Copyright text and illustration © Éditions Flammarion MMIV

ISBN 978-1-907184-74-1

The right of Alain Surget to be identified as the author of this work and the right of
Fabrice Parme to be identified as the illustrator of this work has been asserted in
accordance with sections 77 and 78 of the Copyright, Designs and Patents Act, 1988.

English edition © The Salariya Book Company
& Bailey Publishing Associates MMXI

Printed and bound in China

Translated by Glynne Yeardley

Written by
Alain Surget

Illustrated by
Fabrice Parme

CAESAR, WHO'S HE?

Translated by
Glynne Yeardley

A division of Book House

CONTENTS

CHAPTER 1

NIGHT FISHING

CLEOPATRA'S PALACE
AT ALEXANDRIA, EGYPT, 48 BC

Cleo tiptoed towards the door of Lady Tari's bedroom. She opened it just a crack and listened. She was relieved to hear snoring. That meant that Lady Tari was sleeping like a log. Cleopatra had put Lady Tari in charge of Cleo and she had taken it upon herself to teach the girl to read and write. What a chore that was! Cleo was made to spend the best part of each day deciphering and copying hieroglyphics when she had so many other more important things to do – such as having fun with her friends Imeni and Antinios.

Closing the door again, Cleo walked over to her bedroom window. She pulled back the papyrus-leaf curtain. The night was blue-black. She could see the outlines of the soldiers as they did their circuit of the palace walls. 'I can just do it. By the time they come round again I can be at the other end of the garden,' she thought to herself.

She swung her legs over the windowsill and climbed out onto the branch of an enormous fig tree that grew against the palace wall. She clambered down the trunk to the ground below. Cleo ran along the path as fast as she could to reach a shadowy area behind the palace. She stopped to check that the coast was clear. The guards hadn't got there yet so, taking a deep breath, she dashed to the outer wall that separated the gardens from the street beyond.

Cleo had thought of everything: earlier that day she'd emptied the tools out of an old chest and hidden it in a flower bed. She fumbled around in the darkness, found the chest and dragged it over to the wall. Standing the chest up on its end, she climbed on to it. From this height it was easy to grip hold of the edge of the wall to pull herself up, climb over the top and drop down into the street on the other side.

A shadow slipped out from behind a palm tree. Something hurled itself towards her legs.

She cried out in surprise, but the momentary fear passed as she recognised the desert fox that belonged to her friend Antinios. He came over to her and called the fox back.

'Fenk! Fenk!'

But Fenk didn't obey his master. He carried on nipping at Cleo's ankles until Antinios made a grab for him and held him safely in his arms.

'Where's Imeni?' Cleo asked.

'He's late, as usual.'

'I hope he managed to leave his house without getting caught. Let's go and find him.'

The two children walked along the harbour towards the sea wall that connected the town to the island of Pharos. The streets were deserted apart from one or two men on their way home from the tavern. They weren't far from the agora, the market square, when a small figure appeared round a corner.

'There he is!' cried Antinios as Imeni came to meet them.

'You took your time!' said Cleo.

'You know that my family have only just arrived in Alexandria,' explained the young Egyptian. 'We were sorting things out until really late. Then I had to wait for my parents to fall asleep. But I still don't understand why you want to go fishing at this time of night! It's much easier in daylight! If my father finds out that I've gone fishing at night he'll hit me with his stick.'

'Same for me,' groaned Antinios.

'Night time is much more magical,' said Cleo. 'The sea seems much bigger, so you can't tell if you're sailing on the sea or up in the sky. There's no-one near. You feel as though you're the master of the universe. Don't you feel like that, too?'

'Well yes, of course,' Imeni agreed. 'But…'

'And anyway, it's always much more fun if it's not allowed! What's the point of going fishing in daylight?'

'To catch fish?' the boy suggested. 'At night, fish sleep!'

Cleo shrugged her shoulders. She led the little

group towards the sea wall. That was where the fishermen tied up their small reed boats, whereas the warships and the big trading ships were moored in docks all along the harbour. The three children went down to the sea and climbed into the first boat they came to. They unfastened the rope and with a few paddle strokes left the sea wall behind.

'We'd better steer clear of the area lit by the lighthouse,' said Antinios. 'Imeni and I definitely don't want the guards to see us and take us back home. It doesn't matter to you, Cleo, you are under the queen's protection.'

'You're wrong there,' she said defensively. 'Cleopatra might treat me as if I were her little sister, but I still have to obey Lady Tari. She's in charge of me and she's pretty strict! Okay, stay in the shadows if you want.'

They followed the sea wall until they reached the island of Pharos, then decided to take cover amongst some big rocks. The two boys dropped their lines into the water. Cleo lay back in the boat watching the stars until they seemed to spin around. It made her feel slightly dizzy.

'Someone's coming,' hissed Imeni.

Cleo sat up. He was right. A boat was coming towards them from the sea wall.

'There are three men in it,' murmured Antinios. 'Quick! Lie down in the boat so they don't see us!'

The children lay down as best they could. Imeni practically had Cleo's foot in his mouth and the oars were digging into Antinios.

'No, Fenk!' said Imeni. 'This is no time to play.'

'Shush! They'll hear us.'

They could hear voices across the water. It was hard to make out any words, but they became clearer as the boat got closer to the rocks.

'Here we are,' said one of the men. 'The pirate Shardane is waiting for you. You have made good your escape, General Achillas.'

'Yes, Cleopatra can start to worry now.'

CHAPTER 2

VOICES OVER
THE WATER

The three friends were stunned. Achillas! The very man who'd wanted to kill Cleopatra and seize her throne. Achillas, the traitor that they'd managed to get arrested. So General Achillas had escaped and was now talking of revenge.

The three children flattened themselves down even more as the men's boat came close to the rocks. 'We've got to follow them,' whispered Cleo, 'so we can find out what Achillas is planning.'

'You're mad,' hissed Imeni. 'Didn't you hear? They're going to meet a pirate!'

Antinios risked a quick glimpse over the side. The three men were just disappearing out of sight around the island. Behind them, the town looked peaceful.

'The prison guards can't be aware that he's escaped,' he said. 'Otherwise soldiers would be searching the harbour with torches.'

'So, Achillas is free to lay out his plot without anyone going after him!' exclaimed Cleo. 'I hope you realise that if he plans to kill Cleopatra he will want to get rid of us, too. So we've got to find out what he's up to!'

Antinios agreed. 'Just so long as we keep ourselves hidden.'

To Imeni's great despair, Cleo and Antinios began to paddle away from the rocks. The little boat glided alongside the island and reached the temple of Isis.

'They're near the jetty. I think they're going to land,' he warned them.

'No, I don't think so,' said Cleo. 'They're keeping to the shadows like us but they're heading for that boat just over there.'

She was right. The boat was simply following the jetty until it pulled up alongside a fishing boat. The three men climbed on board. The children's boat drew closer, melting into the darkness to avoid the stretch of water in the middle of the harbour that was lit up by the lighthouse flame. Taking care to muffle the sound of their paddles, Cleo and Antinios manoeuvred their boat alongside the hull of the fishing boat. Fortunately no-one was looking out to sea! The men were too busy congratulating the general on his escape.

The pirate Shardane was sitting on a chest near the front. His long hair was almost white and he had a

huge scar across his bare chest. He was the only man not to stand up when Achillas stood before him.

'I helped you escape,' he rasped. 'Now I want the reward I was promised.'

The general sat down and faced the pirate.

'The gold and the precious stones are in the temple of Isis and in Cleopatra's coffers.'

'We could attack the temple,' suggested Shardane. 'It's unguarded apart from a few priests.'

'No,' Achillas retorted. 'We can do better than that! I want to destroy Alexandria. I want to see the town in ruins. Let it all burn: palace, temples, library…'

'I haven't enough men for that,' replied the pirate. 'With my three ships I could just about block the harbour.'

'I have many allies who will lend me men and warships,' declared the general. 'With your forces and mine combined, we could sink all the ships in the harbour. I shall come back here in three days' time. Our men will spread out through the town. They can keep everything they steal. Your three ships won't have enough room in them to carry off all of Alexandria's treasures. The only thing I'm interested in is Cleopatra's head!'

'Oi! What was that noise?' muttered one of the men suddenly. 'I heard something bump against the side of the hull.'

'Oh, it's nothing. It's just the waves knocking the small boat against the side,' replied another man reassuringly.

Then they heard a whimpering sound like an animal.

'What's that then? A fish yelping?'

Peering over the side of the ship they saw an upturned boat floating alongside it.

'Drive your spears into it. Perhaps someone's hiding underneath!' ordered Shardane.

Thwack! Crash! Thwack! The men struck the boat as hard as they could. Soon, only a few broken

reeds were all that remained of the boat that had carried Cleo and her friends.

'Well?' asked Achillas.

'If any spy was under that boat, he'd be in tiny pieces by now.'

'Good! Now let's get out of the harbour before anyone realises I'm missing,' said the general.

The pirates took up their oars. Splash! Splash! Splash! The oars sent up a shower of water. The fishing boat moved off, towing the small boat that had brought Achillas.

Four heads bobbed to the surface and were tossed about by the waves.

'That was a close thing,' gasped Imeni. 'If we hadn't hidden behind Achillas' boat we would have been skewered like kebabs.'

'It was your fault,' grumbled Cleo. 'What possessed you to stick your finger in Fenk's mouth like that?'

'I was trying to keep him busy,' protested Imeni. 'I was afraid he'd start to whine.'

'Well, you succeeded then,' muttered Antinios.

'Now all we can do is swim for it. I can just imagine what my father will say when I get home, wet through.'

'Oh,' moaned Imeni. 'I hope mine doesn't wake up, either!'

'We can't just go to bed,' cried Cleo. 'We must warn Cleopatra!'

CHAPTER 3

TURNIP HEADS

Carrying their sopping wet sandals, the three children ran back through the harbour to reach the palace.

'There are two guards at the bottom of the staircase. They'll never let us in,' Antinios said.

'Don't forget that I live here,' Cleo reminded them. 'Just watch me – I'll make them jump!'

The two sentries were amazed to see children out in the middle of the night. Especially when they realised they were heading straight for the palace.

'Where are you off to?' asked one of the men.

'I'm coming home,' Cleo told them as she resolutely placed her foot on the first step.

'Oh no you don't!' said one of the guards, holding her back with his spear.

The second one laughed.

'This little froggie has mistaken the palace for her pond.'

Cleo crossed her arms and glared at them: 'I am the Princess Cleo!' she declared.

'Well, there's certainly a Cleo who lives in the royal apartments,' conceded the guard. 'But she's fast asleep. What would she be doing out here at this hour? Sling your hook and take these two toads with you!'

'Have you ever seen Princess Cleo?' she insisted.

'No, but I can imagine that she'd be the very opposite of you: tall, beautiful…'

'And dry!' chuckled the other guard.

'Turnip heads!' Cleo shouted.

The men's expressions changed and they looked quite fierce.

'What did you say?' asked one of them, menacingly.

'They must be deaf, too,' added Imeni. 'We could shout and wake Cleopatra up. She'll let us in!'

The two sentries exchanged looks with one another and made a move to charge at the children, who ran off down the street.

'Don't come back or we'll show you what for!' shouted one of the guards.

Cleo, Antinios and Imeni stopped when they reached the palace gardens.

'Tomorrow, I'll come down those steps in my princess's robes and stamp on their feet!' she swore.

'You can warn the queen, then,' Imeni told her. 'I'm tired. I want to...'

But Cleo interrupted him. 'I can't give her enemies a day's advantage. The queen is supposed to be going away tomorrow, at dawn. We must warn her before that.'

'Well then, we'll just have to get into the palace the same way you got out. We'll have to climb over the wall,' said Antinios.

'But Cleo can just as easily see the queen by herself, since she lives in the palace with Cleopatra,' complained Imeni.

'We made a pact to stay together,' Antinios reminded him. 'And so...'

'Be quiet, you two. Otherwise the soldiers will hear us! If they think we're robbers they'll bid us welcome with arrows.'

'Oh!' said Imeni, terrified.

'I'm just kidding...' said Cleo. She helped the boy climb up into the palm tree that leaned against the palace wall before finishing her sentence: '...they'll just cut off your nose and ears.'

They jumped down one after the other, crossed the garden at a run and hid in the shadow of the palace, whilst the guards were over on the far side.

'The coast's clear,' whispered Cleo. 'It's easy to climb up the fig tree now to reach my bedroom.'

The children climbed the tree in silence and then clambered over the windowsill.

'Now then...' whispered Cleo.

She didn't finish. A heavy hand took hold of the back of her neck and she cried out in terror.

CHAPTER 4

PANTHERA IS WATCHING!

Someone lit an oil lamp. Lady Tari was standing in the middle of the room looking extremely angry. A gigantic servant held Cleo by the scruff of the neck and he had Antinios and Imeni firmly under his other arm.

'This is how you spend your nights,' Lady Tari said furiously. 'Swimming in the harbour with your friends!'

'We weren't swimming. We were fishing,' Imeni corrected her.

'Oh, I see,' said Lady Tari, giving him a stern look. 'So you dive in with the fish and catch them by hand.'

Just then she spotted Fenk stuffed under Antinios' tunic.

'I'll have no animals in this room!' She turned to her servant. 'Get them out of here. And you, Cleo, had better have a wash before you go back to bed.'

'Not until I've spoken to Cleopatra,' protested Cleo, struggling. 'Achillas has escaped. He's planning to attack Alexandria along with pirates.'

'You'll say anything to stop me punishing you.'

'But it's true,' cried Antinios. 'We all heard them.'

'Be off with you,' said Lady Tari, showing them the door.

The huge servant gave Cleo a shove, but before reaching the door, Imeni bumped into a big bronze lamp and knocked it over. It fell to the ground with a crash. Burning oil spread in all directions. Panic stricken, Lady Tari called out for help. The servant let go of the children and smothered the flames with handfuls of soil from the plant pots.

'It's out!' he panted, as shouts arose through the palace. 'There's no need to raise the alarm. But... where are those three kids?'

The three children had slipped out into the

corridor and managed to avoid being seen by the
guards summoned by Lady Tari. The queen's
apartments were at the far end of the gallery. A
soldier was standing guard at the entrance. He
would only move if the queen gave orders. A door
opened and Iros, one of Cleopatra's faithful maids,
peeped out.

'What's all this noise? It's disturbing the queen's
pet panther. She's growling and pacing up and
down the room.'

'Well?' a clear voice rang out behind her. 'Who's
responsible for all this racket?'

'That's done it,' lamented Iros. 'Cleopatra's
awake now.'

Antinios had the wits to call out to her. 'General Achillas has escaped!'

The queen appeared in the doorway immediately.

'You three!' she cried in astonishment. 'So why isn't it the night guard telling me this?'

'No-one else knows yet,' said Cleo. 'We saw General Achillas when we were out fishing in the harbour.'

'In the middle of the night?'

The boys hung their heads with embarrassment, but Cleo said quickly:

'Well… if we'd all stayed at home in bed, you'd never have known what we are about to tell you.'

The officer in charge of the night watch finally arrived. He gave a severe look to the three children responsible for all the noise. Before he could say a word, Cleopatra sent him off to the prison to find out whether the general really had escaped.

'Now I will hear what you have to say,' she said, ushering Cleo, Antinios and Imeni into her private room.

Their story was quite brief and was punctuated by growling from Panthera, the queen's panther. She glared at Fenk as they spoke.

'Go. Get changed whilst we wait for the guard to come back!' Cleopatra ordered. 'Before calling my council together, I will check whether you could be mistaken. And be quiet, you!' she added, tapping the panther's snout.

The night guard soon returned with the prison governor who threw himself on the ground before the queen.

'Two guards have been killed and the prisoner has escaped,' he admitted. 'General Achillas must have had help from inside the palace as well as outside. I've launched…'

Cleopatra wasn't listening. She signalled to her maid. Iros crossed to a gong and struck it several times with a mallet. Outside in the corridor, the queen could hear people running, messengers who had gone to call her generals to an extraordinary meeting.

By the time the generals came into the council chamber, Cleopatra was sitting on her throne, waiting for them. The three children were sitting on the steps in front of her and Panthera was lying next to her like a sphinx. The panther's eyes worried Imeni. He was holding Fenk in his lap and he couldn't decide whether Panthera's burning gaze was fixed on him or the fox. He felt quite uncomfortable and swallowed hard. He tried to hide Fenk in his arms so the panther couldn't see him, but a desert fox has such big ears...

The queen asked Cleo to repeat her story. The girl stood up and described what she and her friends had seen and heard.

'We have three days before they attack,' Cleopatra said. 'I had planned to be away from Alexandria, but now I shall delay my journey.'

'We could block the harbour with our warships,' suggested an officer.

'The pirates will land on the piers. We need to protect them and the sea wall,' said the commander of chariots.

'If they attack through the second port to the west, they'll get straight into the city. From that direction, we have no way to stop them!'

Cleopatra raised her hand for silence. She tapped Panthera again with the other hand to stop her growling. The panther began to swish her tail to and fro instead, her eyes still riveted to Imeni, who heartedly wished he wasn't holding Fenk.

'If we can't prevent the pirates and their allies from getting into our harbours, our strategy must be to stop them getting out again. You must arm all the warships and man them with soldiers. Take them out of Alexandria tomorrow night under cover of darkness. When our enemies attack, our vessels will take them from behind. We shall have the advantage of surprise.'

Relief flooded into their faces. It was an excellent plan.

'We must strike them hard and fast,' declared a general.

'And at exactly the right moment,' added another.

'If your ships arrive late, you may be sure I shall feed all your captains to Panthera.'

To emphasise her words, Cleopatra dropped a veil in front of the panther's nose. Snap! With one bite and hardly moving her head, she devoured the veil. The queen dismissed the council and then turned to the children.

'In many ways you have proved more useful than my own men,' she told them. 'That deserves a reward. I have noticed that you and Panthera can't take your eyes off one another,' she said to Imeni. 'Would you like me to give her to you?'

'N... n... n... no thank you,' replied the boy, his teeth chattering.

CHAPTER 5

A SEA OF FLAMES

The next day, soldiers and sailors were busy in the harbour. As usual, any military activity attracted gangs of children. They watched as weapons and provisions were loaded.

'Achillas and Shardane will be blockaded in the port by our ships,' gloated Antinios.

'Yes! And if they do land, our soldiers will be there to chase them through the streets,' added Cleo. 'Isn't Imeni coming today?'

'His father needs him to set up the stone mason's workshop.'

'Don't forget that Cleopatra has invited you to the palace this evening. We can watch the ships set off in the middle of the night from up on her terrace. You can sleep at the palace.'

'That'll be fantastic. But I have to go home now. I've got to help my father in his olive shop. I can leave Fenk with you, if you like. He can keep you company until this evening.'

Cleo pulled a face and was about to say no, but changed her mind and took Fenk in her arms.

'Why not? He'll liven up my writing lesson. After what happened yesterday, Lady Tari won't dare punish me just yet.'

When evening fell, Imeni and Antinios joined the queen and Cleo for a small informal dinner of twenty-seven courses.

'Twenty-seven!' exclaimed Imeni, hugging his belly after the meal. 'I've never eaten so much.'

'You didn't have to eat everything on your plate,' Cleo reminded him. 'I just nibbled a bit from each one.'

At nightfall, the queen led her young guests onto the terrace to look out over the harbour. The soldiers had already boarded the warships and the sailors were at their oars. Long poles were being used to push the ships off from the quays.

'Will the captains be able to navigate in the dark?' asked Imeni. 'The lighthouse doesn't light up the whole harbour – there are still a lot of dark areas.'

'There are men with lamps at the front of each ship. They will guide each ship's pilot,' explained the queen. 'And men with torches will be stationed all along the sea wall to direct them out to sea.'

'Ah, there they are,' said Antinios, spotting lights flickering on the quayside.

Their torches lit up the darkness, but instead of being spaced out along the line of the quay, they were gathering together near the ships. Cleopatra leaned out over the terrace wall. Cleo suddenly felt the queen become tense.

'What's going on?' asked the queen.

'I suppose the men are talking to the soldiers or the sailors,' said Antinios reassuringly.

'I don't think so. The officers would never allow that.'

Suddenly, flames shot through the air like birds.

Burning arrows were being fired. They landed on the ships, setting fire to the sails and piercing the hulls. Men began to shout.

'We're under attack!' cried the queen.

Her cry brought the night guard running.

'Quick! Send help to the ships immediately!' she ordered.

She leaned out once more to see what was happening in the harbour below.

'The soldiers are trying to put out the fires,' said

Antinios, 'but the flames are already as high as the mast tops.'

'We've been betrayed,' raged Cleopatra. 'Only my council knew of our plans. The traitor must be one of my officers.'

'An old friend of Achillas, perhaps...' suggested Antinios.

'I replaced my councillors and advisors months ago, after Achillas was arrested. I didn't want any of his people near me. But that was obviously not enough. There must still be snakes lurking in the palace.'

'Two ships have collided,' cried Imeni. Soldiers and sailors were jumping into the water.

Suddenly they heard the sound of a dreadful crash. A burning ship had hit the pier.

'The sailors are abandoning their posts to save themselves,' said the queen. 'There's no-one steering the ships. I've lost most of my navy along with any hope of defeating the pirates. The support troops are running down to the harbour,' she murmured, as she saw men pouring out of the palace, 'but it's too late. The enemy has succeeded – its men are already in place throughout the city.'

Cleopatra's face was like thunder when she met with her generals. Her voice shook with rage as she told them:

'There are traitors in our army! Some must still be loyal to Achillas. They have destroyed our navy. How can we fight the enemy now?'

'We shall have to flee, my queen!'

'Flee?' cried Cleopatra indignantly, standing up abruptly as if bitten by a snake. 'A queen does not run away! That's just what my enemies want me to do, so they can seize the throne. We must do all we can to protect the city and its people.'

'My parents – they've only just moved to Alexandria,' Imeni whispered to Cleo. 'They'll wish they were back in Memphis.'

Although he'd only spoken in a whisper, it was enough to draw Cleopatra's attention to the fact that the children had followed her into the council chamber.

'Go,' she told them. 'This is no place for children. We have important things to discuss.'

The three friends left gloomily, but they still managed to hear Cleopatra saying:

'I will send a messenger to the garrison at Memphis to get them to send a thousand charioteers as reinforcements.'

The door closed behind them and they heard no more.

CHAPTER 6

CAESAR?

The next afternoon the three children met up in the palace garden. Cleo had invited them for a swim in the lotus pool. They were having fun, swimming and splashing each other, when Panthera leaned over the edge of the pool. Fenk hid behind a rose bush.

'Shoo!' hissed Imeni, splashing water at her to make her go away.

But the panther settled down comfortably a few moments before Cleopatra herself arrived. The queen sat down on a stone bench in the shade of a vine-covered trellis, motionless as a statue. 'Something must have happened,' thought Cleo. 'When she looks like that, it usually means something has not gone her way'

Cleo climbed out of the water and went to sit on the grass at the queen's feet. For a moment Cleopatra sat in silence. Then she sighed:

'They have killed my messenger. A fisherman found him by the canal with an arrow in his chest. My enemies must be watching all the roads. It's pointless to risk sending out any more riders. I'm beginning to think I have more enemies than friends.'

'Then we're finished,' gasped Cleo.

'I've only one hope left. Caesar!'

'Caesar?' said Cleo. 'Who's he?'

'He is a great Roman general. My spies have informed me that he was leading an expedition to the East. He has returned with his ships and is now anchored in the gulf of Canope, taking on provisions.' Cleopatra turned to see why Panthera was growling. The panther was slapping the water with her paw, trying to reach the boys.

'Panthera!' she cried, calling the creature to her side so that Antinios and Imeni could get out of the pool.

'Would this Roman come and help us?' asked Cleo hesitantly.

'Egypt is rich. I shall offer him gold – a great deal of gold! I shall go to meet Caesar tomorrow in the gulf of Canope.'

'What if his ships have already left?' asked the girl, anxiously.

'Then I shall meet up with them at sea. I will not travel in my litter; I shall use the great royal barge. I shall be surrounded by dancing girls and musicians. That will impress Caesar much more than soldiers. At least, I hope so.'

Her maid Iros was running towards them. From the maid's expression Cleopatra knew that something terrible had happened.

'Pirates...' gasped Iros. 'They're coming into the harbour!'

Cleopatra rushed to the terrace and was horrified to see three pirate ships manoeuvring into position to block the harbour entrance.

'But Achillas said in three days' time,' stammered Cleo.

'Shardane is making his attack a day early. He's probably planning to rob the temples of their treasure before Achillas' allies get here so he won't have to share it with them. I must stay here with my soldiers to defend Alexandria. I will not be able to reach Caesar. In any case, the pirates won't let anyone leave.'

'Do you think they'd stop children going out to fish?' asked Cleo.

'No, they wouldn't worry about...'

Cleopatra didn't finish her sentence. She had just understood what the girl was saying.

'You're thinking of asking the Romans for help instead of me, aren't you?'

'Well yes, at least, all three of us.'

Imeni was so shocked that he nearly choked. Antinios dropped Fenk without realising it. They looked at their friend, willing her to come to her senses, but Cleo ignored them.

'I can't even offer you an escort because that would only draw attention to you,' said Cleopatra sadly.

'We sailed the Nile for four days and nights to come from Memphis to Alexandria,' the girl reminded her. 'So we can easily follow the coast for part of the night. It's more dangerous here in the city than out at sea. What does this Caesar look like?'

The queen smiled at her, her hope reviving.

'I've never met him but I imagine he is tall, strong and very handsome.'

CHAPTER 7

TALL, STRONG AND HANDSOME!

Two of the pirate ships had positioned themselves sideways across the harbour to stop large merchant ships from getting in. A third was moored off the island of Pharos, upon which the temple of Isis stood. Egyptian soldiers ran along the sea wall to repel the pirates, but Shardane and his men had quickly disembarked and had formed themselves into a wall of shields with spears projecting outwards. Meanwhile, another group of pirates had broken into the temple and chased out the priests and priestesses.

A little fishing boat was setting out to sea.

'It's just some children!' cried a black-bearded pirate. 'Have you come to fight us?' he shouted to them, laughing.

'No, we're just going fishing,' answered Antinios, his voice trembling. 'It's easier to catch fish at night.'

'Good idea,' said the pirate. 'That way your parents will have something to eat after we've cleaned 'em out.'

His friends burst out laughing. A huge pirate swung a heavy axe.

'Shall I sink 'em?'

'No,' said the bearded man. 'We'll just grab their fish from them when they get back,' he said under his breath.

The pirate signalled for them to pass through. The three children instinctively ducked their heads down as their little boat passed between the two large ships. Imeni held his breath, half expecting to feel an arrow in his back. Even Fenk felt threatened and hid under Cleo's tunic.

The sea opened up in front of them, golden and shimmering in the evening light.

The next morning the sea was like a mirror. The children had slept briefly on a beach before setting out again. They weren't far from Canope now.

'The gulf is behind those rocks,' said Antinios as the town of Canope appeared along the coast.

It took all their remaining strength to paddle around the headland.

They gasped in amazement at the sight that greeted them. Dozens of ships filled the bay, their sails billowing as they turned on their keels to catch the wind.

'They look like giant eagles ready to fly,' marvelled Cleo.

'We've arrived just in time. The ships are ready to leave.'

The three rows of oars beating rhythmically on either side of each ship made the sea around them boil. Cleo stood up and waved her arms furiously at the leading ship, trying to attract the Romans' attention.

'Get in front of it,' she ordered. 'And we'll all shout to Caesar as loud as we can!'

'But we'll be run down!' cried Imeni in terror.

'No, Cleo's right. We'll have to make it stop,' agreed Antinios.

Their little boat was directly in front of the ship. The children waved and yelled at the tops of their voices, trying to be heard above the sound of the oars.

'Cleopatra has sent us! We must speak to Caesar! Caesar!'

'Perhaps he's not on that ship,' observed Imeni.

'He must be!' declared Cleo. 'A general always leads his troops from the front. Come on, shout!'

The captain heard their cries. He leaned over and saw the children waving at him. He slowed the ship so as not to run them down.

'What do you want?' he shouted back.

In a few words, Cleo explained that Alexandria was under siege from pirates. The captain wasn't convinced, but gave them the benefit of the doubt and let them come aboard. Three of the sailors held out their oars to form a sort of ladder. One after another Cleo, Imeni and Antinios climbed onto the ship.

'What's going on?' a man's voice cried angrily. Who gave permission to stop the ship?'

'It's Caesar!' breathed Cleo to her two companions. 'Look how tall he is. How strong and handsome! His armour looks like silver.'

She stepped towards the Roman, bowing her head to show humility.

'Queen Cleopatra seeks your help, oh Caesar. Alexandria…'

'I am not Caesar,' the man interrupted her. 'My name is Mark Antony. That's Caesar wearing the red cloak.'

Cleo was thunderstruck. 'Him?' she murmured to herself. 'But he's old and skinny and looks as dry as a stick under that cloak. That's not how I imagined Caesar...'

She completely forgot to bow to him. Caesar came over and stood in front of her. For a few moments he didn't say a word as his grey eyes studied her intently. At last he spoke:

'You claim to be the queen's envoy? Is Egypt reduced to sending children instead of officers?'

Cleo explained again. Caesar thought about it for a moment, chin in hand.

'These pirates are a real scourge,' he said. 'We must cleanse the sea of them. But Egypt's troubles are not mine. Why should I help Cleopatra deal with this pirate and his henchmen?'

'Because she is the queen, of course!' retorted Cleo, stamping her foot.

Caesar glared at her. No-one had ever spoken to him like that except this little girl. The boys were watching his expression and thought he was about to have them thrown overboard. Or perhaps he'd have the three of them strung up by their ankles from the mast! Antinios tried to mollify Caesar by saying:

'Cleopatra will shower gold on those who comes to her aid.'

'That's right,' urged Imeni.

Caesar did not reply. His eyes leapt from one to the other before coming to rest on the girl again.

'Who are you?'

'I am Cleo, Cleopatra's little sister!' she boasted, folding her arms and striking a rather provocative pose.

The boys looked at each other, stunned. 'What's come over her?' thought Antinios.' 'She must be mad. Caesar will never swallow that.' He could already see the Roman frowning.

'Of course you are. And I suppose those two are Ramses II and Alexander the Great! I don't believe a word of it! You and your friends just wanted to have a closer look at a Roman ship and you've made up all these lies to get on board.'

'No, no!' cried the children. 'Cleopatra sent us – she did, really!'

'We've wasted enough time,' Caesar declared. 'I intended to visit Alexandria anyway, to meet the queen of Egypt. We shall therefore stop at the port as planned. If the city is really under attack, I shall defend it.'

'It might be wise to avoid the city,' put in Mark Antony. 'We shouldn't risk our soldiers' lives in a battle that has nothing to do with us. Our men are exhausted from the Eastern campaign and all they want is to get back to their families. They haven't seen them in ages.'

'I command this fleet!' growled Caesar. 'I shall go to Alexandria and I intend to greet Cleopatra whether the town is in flames or not. It is important for Rome to have good relations with Egypt. The Nile delta could be an important base for our fleet to keep an eye on the East and to supply us with wheat.'

'As you wish,' agreed Mark Antony sullenly. 'Then allow me to return to Rome with some of our army.'

'Certainly not! I am the victorious general. I shall be the one who leads the army back in triumph before my people. I will not allow you to receive Rome's praises instead of me.'

'What do you want me to do with this lot?' asked the captain, pointing to the children. 'Shall I throw them overboard?'

Julius Caesar's gaze returned to the children. He

had almost forgotten them. He bent down, frowning deliberately.

'If I find you have lied to me, I shall take you to Rome and feed you to the lions,' he told them.

Cleo wasn't impressed.

'I don't believe you,' she said.

'Really? And why not?'

'Cleopatra trusts you. So you can't really be that nasty.'

Caesar was forced to smile. He turned to the ship's captain.

'Have the men row at double speed. Egypt awaits me!'

CHAPTER 8

THE GREAT BATTLE

Alexandria was in flames. Since early afternoon, General Achillas' ships had joined the pirate ships blockading the harbour. The queen's soldiers were trying to repel the attackers.

A low rumble was heard through the town. People looked upwards for signs of a storm, but the sky was a cloudless blue. Suddenly, they realised that the thunderous sounds came from the sea. The surprise was absolute: the Roman fleet was just outside the harbour of Alexandria.

At a signal from Caesar, the soldiers stopped beating their war drums and formed into two lines. Then catapults fixed to the front of the ships were uncovered. Zing! Zing! Zing! Each huge machine hurled a great fireball upwards in an enormous arc, far ahead of them. The fireballs burst onto the decks of both the pirate's ships and their allies'.

Panic broke out on the enemy ships and men rushed about trying, unsuccessfully, to put out the fires. Many jumped overboard, trying to save themselves.

'What's burning over yonder?' asked Caesar, looking at the flames rising over the city.

'It's the library,' Cleo told him. 'The pirates must have set fire to it when they didn't find any gold there.'

'I just hope that the fire doesn't destroy the whole area!' cried Antinios. 'That's where my family live!'

'Cease firing!' ordered Caesar. 'We'll smash up what's left of their ships now.'

The Roman ships were armed with huge bronze rams fixed to their prows. They advanced on the pirate ships, shearing off oars and smashing holes in their hulls. Once the harbour was clear of all but a few smoking remnants of wreckage, Caesar ordered his men to disembark.

'Mark Antony, you take half of the troops to reinforce those soldiers fighting on the shore. I'll take care of the area around the palace. As for you three,' he said, turning to the children, 'stay here on board my ship. You will be safe here.'

The legionaries climbed down to the quayside and, with sword and shield in hand, set off behind their officers.

'If Caesar thinks we're just going to stay here like good little children...' grumbled Cleo quietly so that only her friends could hear.

'What are you hatching now?' demanded Imeni. 'Surely you're not planning to go and fight Achillas or Shardane, are you?

'I want to know what's happening at the palace. Cleopatra might be wounded or worse. Remember that Achillas planned to kill her!'

'You won't be able to change the course of... Hey!' shouted Antinios, as if his cry would stop Cleo as she jumped onto the gangplank.

'Oi! 'cried Imeni, losing his hold on Fenk as the fox went bounding after her. 'What'll we do?'

'We'll have to go after them!' decided Antinios.

One of the sailors spotted them running along the quayside and alerted the captain, who shrugged his shoulders. It was too bad. He was responsible for the ship, not those who got off it.

The harbour was deserted so Cleo, Imeni and Antinios had no trouble in reaching the palace. The gates had been smashed open and bodies were strewn across the steps.

'Caesar's men are still fighting at the entrance,' remarked Antinios as he heard shouting and the clash of swords.

'Let's go through the garden,' suggested Cleo.

'There are pirates everywhere,' said Imeni. 'We'll get ourselves killed.'

But Cleo took no notice of him. She dashed down the street that ran alongside the garden wall, with Antinios and Fenk hard on her heels.

'Wait for me! Wait for me!' Imeni yelled.

Suddenly, a man appeared round the corner of a house, right in front of Cleo. They froze in shock for a moment before recognising one another. It was the black-bearded pirate who had let them go fishing in their boat.

'Hah!' he sneered, making a grab for the girl. 'I didn't see you come back last night and now here you are – at the same time as the Romans!'

He held Cleo by the neck and pulled a dagger out from his belt, ready to cut her throat. A sharp pain in his ankle suddenly stopped him in his tracks. He shook his leg to get rid of the fox hanging on to it. Cleo hit him on the nose and escaped. Antinios punched him hard in the stomach whilst Imeni kicked him in the knee, breaking his kneecap.

The pirate collapsed, yelling and clutching his leg. The children, meanwhile, climbed up the palm tree to the top of the wall and jumped down into the royal gardens.

Some of the maids and man-servants were hiding behind hedges and up in the tree tops whilst others hid beneath the lily pads in the pond. One old woman recognised Cleo and warned her not to go any further.

'Where is the queen?' demanded Cleo. 'Did she get away from Achillas?'

'No-one has seen her. No-one knows where she is. Cleopatra has disappeared!'

CHAPTER 9

WHERE'S CLEOPATRA?

Inside the palace, the pirates and their allies were putting up a fierce resistance against the Romans. They were gradually driven back and had to drop their booty to escape with their lives.

'Search the corridors!' Caesar ordered his legionaries. 'Attack the enemy from all sides. Block off the gardens as well. These riff-raff mustn't be allowed to get away.'

'You must find Cleopatra!' he reminded his officers as they were about to lead their men through the palace.

Whilst his troops began searching the palace, Caesar set off to the throne room with another party of men. The doors were wide open. Shardane and his pirates were stuffing all the treasure they could find into chests. They were greatly surprised by Caesar's arrival. Some panicked and didn't know which way to turn. Shardane gave a loud battle cry and, brandishing his sword, launched himself at the Romans.

A legionary stepped in front of Caesar in order to protect him. The pirate's weapon bounced off his shield. A second soldier wounded Shardane in the leg with his sword. A third struck him in the heart.

'The queen isn't here,' said Caesar. 'Deal with these thieves and join me in the royal apartments!'

The soldiers threw themselves at the pirates, whilst Caesar went back up the corridor with an escort of a dozen men. Their footsteps rang out on the flagstones. They turned a corner and suddenly came upon General Achillas and an Egyptian officer. As soon as he saw Caesar, Achillas killed the officer. The man collapsed across a large chest. The Romans reached him as he sheathed his sword.

'I am in charge of security,' Achillas lied. 'My men are all dead, having put up a valiant struggle.'

'And who is that?' asked Caesar, pointing to the Egyptian officer's body.

'That was the queen's night guard. A traitor and an ally of Achillas who was trying to steal some treasure.'

'Where is Achillas?'

'He went out over the terrace. I was chasing him when his accomplice here tried to stop me.'

Caesar gave an order to his men and they rushed off in the direction he was pointing. Achillas pushed the night guard off the chest and opened it. Headdresses, bracelets and necklaces studded with precious stones sparkled from within.

'This is worth a fortune,' he said.

'Where is Cleopatra?' asked Caesar.

'I really don't know.' The general appeared genuinely regretful. 'I asked her to lock herself in her room when the attack began.'

'Then take me to her chamber!' ordered Caesar.

'There's no point. I have been told she is no longer there.'

'You say you are responsible for the queen's safety and yet you have no idea where she has gone? Does she have any servants she can depend on? Take me to her chamber anyway.'

The two men glared at one another. Caesar indicated that Achillas should go ahead of him to lead the way. The general thought it wise to comply. Then he had an idea.

'This is it,' declared Achillas, opening the doors to the royal apartments. But the room was empty.

Caesar stepped inside the room. Achillas

followed and closed the door behind him. The Roman stood in the middle of the room with his hands on his hips, admiring the magnificent paintings that covered the walls.

'Caesar has his back to me. It's now or never,' Achillas decided. He placed his hand on the hilt of his sword and slowly drew it from its scabbard. Suddenly there was a shout.

'That's Achillas! Caesar, that's Achillas!'

Caesar instantly turned and ducked. The traitor's weapon whistled over his head. Caesar's

dagger caught Achillas in the side. The general fell to the ground.

'I had my suspicions,' muttered Caesar. 'That chest was far too big for one man to be carrying. But that voice... I recognise it.'

Cleo, standing on Antinios and Imeni's shoulders, was holding onto the window ledge. Caesar held out his hand and pulled her inside.

'You have a very strange way of coming into your sister's room,' he said, smiling. 'But I shan't complain this time.'

Antinios appeared next and Cleo helped pull him up. Then they both hoisted Imeni inside. Caesar sniffed as if he could smell the queen's perfume.

'Where is Cleopatra?' he demanded.

Shadows appeared on the wall, followed by two figures that emerged from secret niches hidden on either side of the door. Cleopatra's maidservants bowed before the Roman.

'The queen is here amongst us.'

'Really?' said Caesar. 'Is it one of you?'

The two women went over to a rolled carpet and, with one at each end, gave it a push and unrolled it towards Caesar to reveal – Cleopatra! The queen stood up, stunning in her white linen dress. Caesar stood open mouthed. Here was the queen without her crown and jewels or anything else to distract his eye. He saw, before him, a very beautiful woman with a dazzling smile.

'The carpet was our idea,' whispered Imeni to Antinios.

Cleopatra gave the children a conspiratorial wink before turning to Caesar.

'I thank you for coming to help me. Egypt will shower her gratitude on Rome.'

He held out his arm to her. The queen accepted and together, they stepped over Achillas' body and left the room.

'Give me your hands, boys!' ordered Cleo as if she were a queen. 'I want to walk like a princess, too.'

Unlike Cleopatra however, Cleo couldn't resist giving Achillas a quick kick as she walked to the door.

Alexandria licked its wounds. The fire in the library had been put out before the papyrus rolls had been enveloped in flames. Those pirates and their allies who had survived the fighting had been captured and imprisoned. As for Achillas, he had been left for dead in the queen's chamber, but he'd not been fatally wounded. He'd managed to escape before the servants came to remove his body. The Roman fleet sailed, leaving behind Julius Caesar, whom the queen had invited to stay in Egypt for as long as he wanted.

On the evening after the victory, Cleo, Antinios and Imeni were standing on the terrace overlooking the harbour. The sun was slipping into the sea leaving only lighthouse flame to illuminate the water.

'If it wasn't for us, the sea would be red tonight,' declared Imeni. 'It would have been the flames of Alexandria that lit up the sky.'

'It's a pity that Achillas escaped,' sighed Cleo. 'He killed his accomplice to fool Caesar, but he may still have other allies amongst Cleopatra's people. We'll have to keep our eyes and ears open.'

'Between the three of us we'll foil any plots,' said Antinios confidently. 'Just as long as we always stick together!'

He held out his hand, palm down. Cleo placed her hand on top of it, followed by Imeni. A fourth hand then rested on top of his. They turned to see... Cleopatra!

'You can count me in, too,' said the queen.

'Between the four of us, we shall defend Egypt from any enemy.'

ABOUT THE AUTHOR

Alain Surget is a professor of history as well as a prolific novelist. He started writing plays and poetry at the early age of 14, then went on to write over 130 novels and other books. His first sight of the Pyramids and images of the Pharaohs sparked a lifelong interest in Ancient Egypt. Many of his novels are set there.

Alain is married with three children and lives in Gap in France. Despite writing about the adventures and travels of his characters – who are often feisty heroines – Alain admits to being an armchair traveller himself!

ABOUT THE ILLUSTRATOR

Fabrice Parme was born near Nancy in France. After finishing Art School in Angoulême, he moved to Paris where he worked as an illustrator for various magazines, including comic and 'graphic novel' style, and for television. His illustrations for the Children of the Nile series are the first he has done for children's books.

www.salariya.com
where books come to life!

Follow us on Facebook and Twitter

Children's non-fiction and graphic novels

Fiction for children and teenagers

The Book House blog - competitions, giveaways and current news

www.youtube.com/user/BookHouse100

FREE APP!

FREE WEB BOOK!

FREE WEB BOOKS!

Download our free iPhone and iPad catalogue app. Go to http://bit.ly/c8zQuy or search for Salariya at the App Store

Four free web books